Horse Up a Tree

Written by Martin Waddell
Illustrated by Jonathan Allen

Collins

One day Horse went up a tree ...
... and got stuck.

The ducks and the hens and the sheep ran
to the tree to help Horse.
Quack-quack! Cluck-cluck! Baa-baa!

Farmer came with a ladder.
"Get on the ladder!" Farmer said to Horse.

They all got on the ladder to show
Horse what to do.
Quack-quack! Cluck-cluck! Baa-baa!

Horse looked at the ground far below.
Horse shook his mane and said **nay!**

Farmer hung a rope from a branch.
"Swing on the rope!" Farmer said to Horse.

They all swung on the rope to show
Horse what to do.
Quack-quack! Cluck-cluck! Baa-baa!

Horse looked at the ground far below.
Horse shook his mane and said **nay!**

Farmer got some hay.
"Jump on the hay!" Farmer said to Horse.

They all jumped on the hay to show
Horse what to do.
Quack-quack! Cluck-cluck! Baa-baa!

Horse looked at the ground far below.
Horse shook his mane and said **nay!**

"One last try ... *do not look at the ground,*
just hop on the branch!" Farmer said to Horse.

10

They all hopped about to show
Horse what to do.
Quack-quack! Cluck-cluck! Baa-baa!

This time Horse did not say **nay!**
He looked up at the sky as he hopped and ...
CRACK!
The branch broke...

... and they all landed in the hay.